The Pig Who Ran a Red Light

PAUL BRETT JOHNSON

The Pig
Who Ran
a Red Light

ORCHARD BOOKS   NEW YORK

Orchard Books, A Grolier Company
95 Madison Avenue, New York, NY 10016

Manufactured in the United States of America
Printed and bound by Phoenix Color Corp.
Book design by Kristina Albertson
The text of this book is set in 15 point Esprit Medium.
The illustrations are watercolor.
10 9 8 7 6 5 4 3 2 1

Library of Congress Cataloging-in-Publication Data
Johnson, Paul Brett. The pig who ran a red light / Paul Brett Johnson.
p.   cm. Summary: After her pig George gets a ticket while driving her pickup truck,
Miss Rosemary uses his habit of imitating Gertrude the cow to get him to behave
as he should.
ISBN 0-531-30136-2 (trade : alk. paper).—ISBN 0-531-33136-9 (lib. bdg. : alk. paper)
[1. Pigs—Fiction. 2. Domestic animals—Fiction.] I. Title.
PZ7.J6354Pi   1999   [E]—dc21   98-36161

For those who have sometimes
wished to be somebody else

Ever since Gertrude had taken up flying,
there had been no living with George.

"Weeeeee!" came a sudden high squeal.
Miss Rosemary made it to the kitchen door in time
to see her pig take a run-and-go off the end of the porch.

FFOOOMP!

Miss Rosemary shook her head. "Honestly, George! Just because Gertrude is a silly nincompoop, doesn't mean you have to be one too. It's a known fact pigs don't fly. Now look what you've done to my petunias."

George was not about to listen to reason, however. The minute Gertrude fired up the old farm tractor, he climbed behind the wheel of Miss Rosemary's pickup.

George smashed through the chicken coop,
squished over the pumpkin patch, bounced across
the creek, and chugged off down U.S. 80 on the
wrong side of the road.

"Heaven help us all!" Miss Rosemary cried as she
ran to the phone and called the sheriff. "This is an
emergency!" she said. "My pig is driving on the
wrong side of the road!"

"Now don't you worry about a thing, ma'am," said the sheriff. "We'll take care of the situation." But when he hung up, he lifted his eyebrows and tapped his head. "Lady says her pig is driving on the wrong side of the road. Heh, heh."

However, it wasn't long until the sheriff
saw George with his own eyes!

He had to give George a ticket for running a red light and driving without a license. He then called Miss Rosemary to come get her pig.

"What am I going to do with you, George?" Miss Rosemary scolded. "It's a known fact pigs don't drive. Why do you have to act like Gertrude? Why can't you just be yourself?"

When George and Miss Rosemary got back home,
Gertrude was practicing the piano.

George joined in.

"George, you are going to send me to the loony bin!"
Miss Rosemary shouted above the noise.

There was no doubt about it: *something* had to be done.

Miss Rosemary had a long talk with Gertrude—just
the two of them.

The following day at lunch, Miss Rosemary rang the bell. *CLANG! CLANG! CLANG!* "Who wants a big slice of apple pie?" she called.

Gertrude came running. George was close behind. "OINK! OINK!" said Gertrude.

George stopped dead in his tracks. He cocked his
head and looked at Gertrude.

After lunch, Gertrude went to the barnyard. She stuck her nose to the ground and began rooting and snorting. She even managed to curl her tail. "OINK, OINK," she said again.

George was speechless.

Later that afternoon, Miss Rosemary hooked up the garden hose and made a huge pit of yucky, mucky, black, stinky mud.

"Anyone for a wallow?" Miss Rosemary asked.

Gertrude jumped—*kersplat!*—into the yucky, mucky pit. She rolled over and over. She tossed globs of mud into the air. "OINK, OINK!" squealed Gertrude, pretending to be in hog heaven.

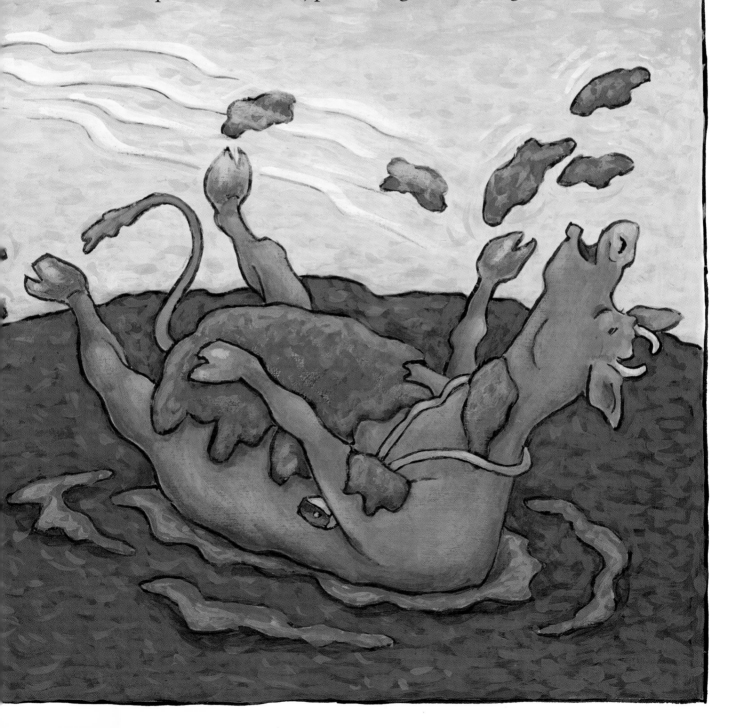

Suddenly George screamed like a fire engine.
"Weeeeeeeeeeeee!"
Into the pit he went.

Miss Rosemary sighed thankfully. At last, her
pig was behaving like a pig.

"Cows are cows, and pigs are pigs," said Miss
Rosemary. "And that's a known fact."

"OINK, OINK," said George.

"OINK, OINK," said Gertrude.

"OINK, OINK," said Magnolia.

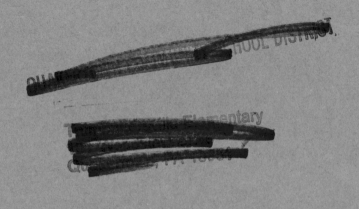